This
Bear with Sticky Paws
book belongs to:

. . . .

KEEP YOUR PAWS OFF!

for Stephanie with love x

ORCHARD BOOKS
338 Euston Road, London NW1 3BH
Orchard Books Australia
Level 17/207 Kent Street, Sydney, NSW 2000

First published in 2010
by Orchard Books
First published in paperback in 2011
Text and illustrations © Clara Vulliamy 2010

A CIP catalogue record for this book
is available from the British Library.

ISBN 978 1 40830 065 7
1 3 5 7 9 10 8 6 4 2
Printed in China
Orchard Books is a division of Hachette Children's Books,
an Hachette UK company.
www.hachette.co.uk

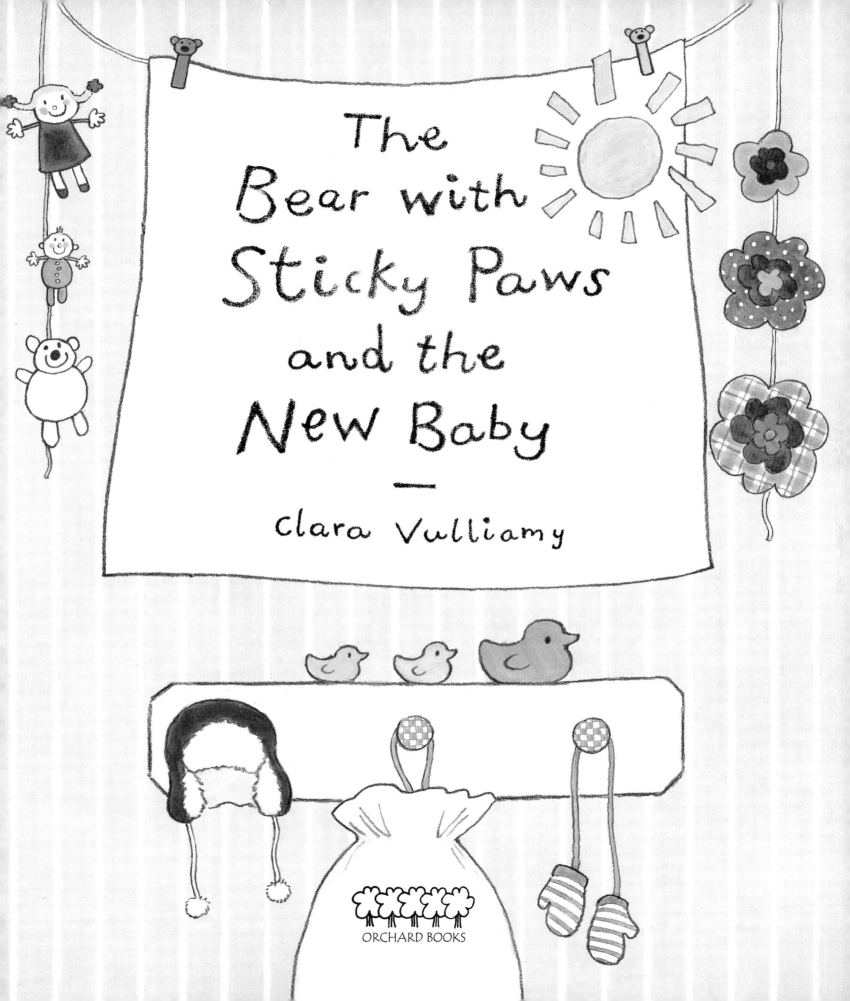

The Bear with Sticky Paws and the New Baby

Clara Vulliamy

ORCHARD BOOKS

There's a girl called Pearl
with a new baby brother.
She says,

"That's my high chair,

I'm still

VERY SMALL!"

"Come and sit at the table properly," says Mum.
"You're my special grown-up girl."

"I'm **not** grown-up!

Look at me, look at me –

I'm a baby, too!"

But then,

bing-

bong!

There's a bear on the doorstep,
a small white tufty one,
standing on his suitcase to reach the bell.

"Grown-up?" says the bear.
"Boring!
Let's play BABY BEARS!"

"I'm hungry!" says the bear,
squeezing into the high chair.
"FEED ME!"

"Spoons? Not spoons!" says the bear.

"Baby bears use their PAWS!"

"Well, I use a spoon," says Pearl.

The bear eats

9 squashy bananas

8 jars of baby food

and 7 bowls of mush.

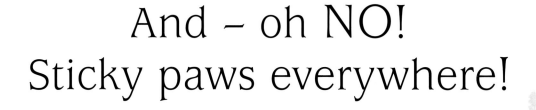

And – oh NO!
Sticky paws everywhere!

But baby bears don't care . . .

now they're
rolling and crawling,

tumbling and
tickling,

giggling and chasing . . .

"Baby clothes!"

says the bear.

The bear chooses

6 small hats

5 tiny vests

and 4 teeny socks.

"DRESS ME!" says the bear.

"I dress myself," says Pearl.

"OUTSIDE!" says the bear.

"It's swing-time!"

"PUSH ME!
Higher, higher, higher!"

"I can swing myself,"
says Pearl.

"I'm tired," says the bear. "CARRY ME!"

"You're SO heavy," says Pearl.

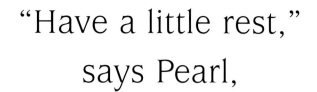

"Have a little rest,"
says Pearl,

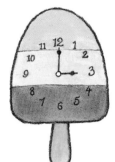

"while I look at
books."

"No more rest for baby bears!"

says the bear.

"I want to do some drawing,"
says Pearl.

"Not drawing," says the bear,

"Baby bears do SCRIBBLING!"

The bear does

3 blue scribbles

2 red scribbles

and 1 HUGE multicoloured scribble.

And – oh NO!
Sticky paws everywhere!

"Let's play a game,"
says Pearl.
"Animal pairs?"

"Building a tower?"

"Baby bears don't do animal pairs! Baby bears like to KNOCK THINGS DOWN!

Look at ME, look at ME!"

"ME!"

"ME!"

"ME!"

Until Pearl calls out . . .

"STOP!"

"No more baby bears!" says Pearl.
"I want to be a grown-up girl today."

"Goodbye!"

"Goodbye!"

"Mum, I made this for the baby!"
says Pearl.

"What a lucky baby,"
says Mum . . .

"... to have such a lovely sister."